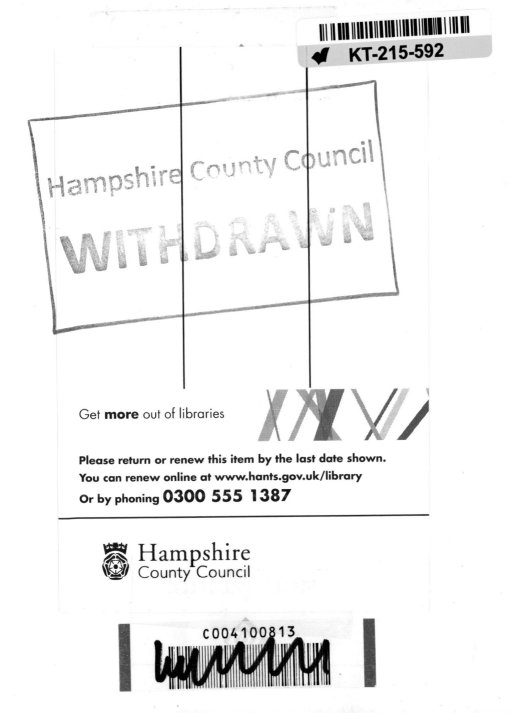

Get **more** out of libraries

Please return or renew this item by the last date shown.
You can renew online at www.hants.gov.uk/library
Or by phoning **0300 555 1387**

Hampshire
County Council

First published in 2005 by
Franklin Watts
96 Leonard Street
London
EC2A 4XD

Franklin Watts Australia
45–51 Huntley Street
Alexandria
NSW 2015

A CIP catalogue record for this book is available
from the British Library.

ISBN 0 7496 6126 7 (hbk)
ISBN 0 7496 6132 1 (pbk)

**Series Editor:** Jackie Hamley
**Series Advisors:** Dr Barrie Wade, Dr Hilary Minns
**Design:** Peter Scoulding


Printed in Hong Kong / China

For my godchildren – Max, Izzy, Walter and Jessica – J.A.

# The Great Escape

Written by
**Sue Graves**

Illustrated by
**Jane Abbott**

W
FRANKLIN WATTS
LONDON•SYDNEY

**Sue Graves**

"I hope you enjoy this book. It is based on a true story. I bet the farmer was very surprised!"

**Jane Abbott**

"I live in the countryside and there are lots of sheep about. I haven't seen any of them rolling past yet, but I think they're learning!"

Susan and Sarah were sisters.

They lived in a field

on Daisy Farm.

The sisters didn't like their field much. They wanted to escape to the next field.

"That field's much better than ours," Sarah said.

But they couldn't escape because
they couldn't get over the grid!

They tried getting over in lots of
ways. They tried walking across.

Then they tried jumping across.

13

They even tried tiptoeing
across! But each time they
got stuck.

16

Then Sarah had a good idea. "Let's roll across the grid," she said. "We won't get stuck if we roll across."

So Sarah rolled herself into a ball. She rolled across into the next field.

whee!

"Come on, Susan," said Sarah.
"It's easy!" Susan rolled herself
into a ball.

She rolled across into the
next field, too.

*whee!*

"What a lovely field!" said Susan.

"Lovely," agreed Sarah.

lovely field!

Suddenly, Susan heard snorting
and stamping. She looked round.

A big bull was in the field.

He had seen the sheep.

The big bull charged at them.

"Run for it, Sarah!" cried Susan.

They ran to the grid.

They rolled right over and back
into their own field.

"What a lovely field!" said Sarah.
"Lovely," said Susan. "This field's
the best one of all!"

# Notes for parents and teachers

READING CORNER has been structured to provide maximum support for new readers. The stories may be used by adults for sharing with young children. Primarily, however, the stories are designed for newly independent readers, whether they are reading these books in bed at night, or in the reading corner at school or in the library.

Starting to read alone can be a daunting prospect. READING CORNER helps by providing visual support and repeating words and phrases, while making reading enjoyable. These books will develop confidence in the new reader, and encourage a love of reading that will last a lifetime!

If you are reading this book with a child, here are a few tips:

**1.** Make reading fun! Choose a time to read when you and the child are relaxed and have time to share the story.

**2.** Encourage children to reread the story, and to retell the story in their own words, using the illustrations to remind them what has happened.

**3.** Give praise! Remember that small mistakes need not always be corrected.

READING CORNER covers three grades of early reading ability, with three levels at each grade. Each level has a certain number of words per story, indicated by the number of bars on the spine of the book, to allow you to choose the right book for a young reader:

| GRADE 1 | GRADE 2 | GRADE 3 |
|---------|---------|---------|
| 50 words | 130 words | 250 words |
| 70 words | 160 words | 350 words |
| 100 words | 200 words | 450 words |